Andrew Murray

The Very Sleepy Sloth

Jack Tickle

TED SMART

Deep in the jungle,
early in the morning,
the sloth was fast asleep.

But the rest of
the animals were
wide awake.

The cheetah was on
the running machine,
working on his

SPEED.

The elephant was
lifting heavy weights,
working on her

STRENGTH.

The kangaroo was
on the trampoline,
working on her

SPRING.

The monkey was
on the high bars,
working on his

SWING.

While the sloth stayed
in his hammock,
working on his sleep.

"That sloth is so lazy,"
said Cheetah.

"All he does is lie there!"
agreed Elephant.

"Just dozing in his hammock,"
added Kangaroo.

"Hey, Sloth!" called Monkey.
"We're all working hard here.
Why don't you get up and
do something?"

Sloth slowly opened one eye.
"Monkey," he said. "If you're
so hard-working, you try
lifting Elephant's weights."

"Easy!" said Monkey,
and he tried to lift
the weights.
Elephant giggled as . . .

oooooof!

Monkey toppled
right over.

"Elephant!"
said Monkey gruffly.
"If you think it's so easy,
you jump like Kangaroo!"

So Elephant tried to
jump on the trampoline.
Kangaroo tutted as . . .

CRASH!

Elephant fell right through.
"Don't tut at me, Kangaroo!"
said Elephant grumpily.
"Can *you* run like Cheetah?"

So Kangaroo tried
the running machine.
Cheetah chuckled as
Kangaroo landed on . . .

So Cheetah climbed
the high bars and
swung right into . . .

Elephant.

EEEEE EK!

By now, everyone was very hot,
very tired and very, very cross.

"This is useless," they muttered.
"Who caused all this trouble?"

"It wasn't me," said Cheetah.
"I was busy running."

"It wasn't me," said Kangaroo.
"I was busy bouncing."

"It wasn't me," said Elephant.
"I was busy lifting weights."

"And it wasn't me," said Monkey.
"I was busy swinging."

All the animals turned
and looked at . . .

SLOTH!

"Hey, Sloth," they called.
"You started this!"

Sloth turned lazily.
"You must see by now,"
he said. "We were all busy doing
what we do best. Even me!"

The animals thought about it.
"Yes!" they cried. "We're all good at
running or jumping or lifting or swinging.
But Sloth is the very best at . . .

OZING!"

"Exactly!" said Sloth.
And with a stretch
and a yawn he fell
fast asleep!

For Joyce, Ashifa and everyone
at Ottakar's Bromley
~A.M.

For Jazz
~J.T.

This edition produced for
The Book People Ltd
Hall Wood Avenue, Haydock,
St Helens WA11 9UL, by
LITTLE TIGER PRESS
1 The Coda Centre, 189 Munster Road,
London SW6 6AW
www.littletigerpress.com

First published in Great Britain 2003

A CIP catalogue record for this book
is available from the British Library

Printed in Belgium by Proost NV

1 2 3 4 5 6 7 8 9 10